P9-BZC-197

Wauconda Area Library
801 N. Main Street
Wauconda, IL 60084

Horses

Trotting! Prancing! Racing!

by **Patricia Hubbell**

illustrated by **Joe Mathieu**

Marshall Cavendish Children

Wauconda Area Library
801 N. Main Street
Wauconda, IL 60084

Special thanks go to Sharon Lerner and Susan Jeffers, horse experts, who were so generous with their time and expertise. Thanks also to Bernie Samson of Samson Harness Shop for his technical knowledge and enthusiasm.

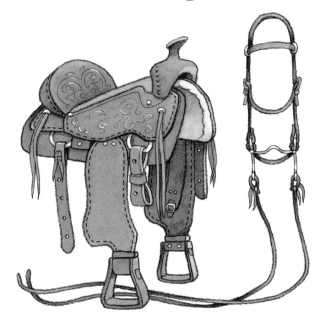

Text copyright © 2011 by Patricia Hubbell
Illustrations copyright © 2011 by Joe Mathieu

All rights reserved

Marshall Cavendish Corporation, 99 White Plains Road, Tarrytown, NY 10591
www.marshallcavendish.us/kids

Library of Congress Cataloging-in-Publication Data
Hubbell, Patricia.
Horses : Trotting! Prancing! Racing! / by Patricia Hubbell ; illustrated
by Joe Mathieu. — 1st ed.
p. cm.
Summary: Rhyming verses describe how horses work, rest, and play. Includes
illustrated list of horse breeds.
ISBN 978-0-7614-5949-1 (hardcover) — ISBN 978-0-7614-5997-2 (ebook)
[1. Stories in rhyme. 2. Horses—Fiction.] I. Mathieu, Joseph, ill. II.
Title.
PZ8.3.K46Ho 2011
[E]—dc22
2010044929

The illustrations are rendered in Winsor & Newton watercolors, Luma watercolors, Prismacolor pencils,
and Derwent pencils on Arches cold press paper.

Book design by Vera Soki
Editor: Marilyn Brigham

Printed in China (E)
First edition
10 9 8 7 6 5 4 3 2 1

Marshall Cavendish
Children

For Deb and all of our wonderful ponies and horses, past and present,
especially Tiny and Billy
—P.H.

To Sharon Lerner, who has been such a good friend for so many years,
and to her beautiful horse, Coda
—J.M.

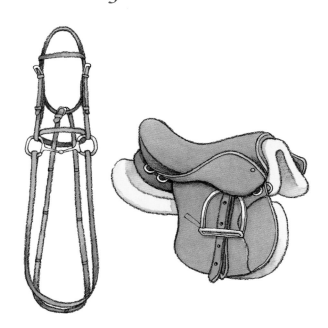

Big horses. Small horses.
Stamping-in-the-stall horses.

Whinny! Snort! Nicker! Neigh!
Time for breakfast—grain and hay.

Clean their stalls! Fill their pails!
Brush their bodies, manes, and tails.

Wipe their ears. Shine their feet.
Give them apples for a treat.

A horse can be black, brown, or bay,
palomino, chestnut, gray,

have freckles, streaks, and polka dots,
be black and white with splotchy spots.

Horses buck and roll and snooze.

Some of them wear iron shoes.

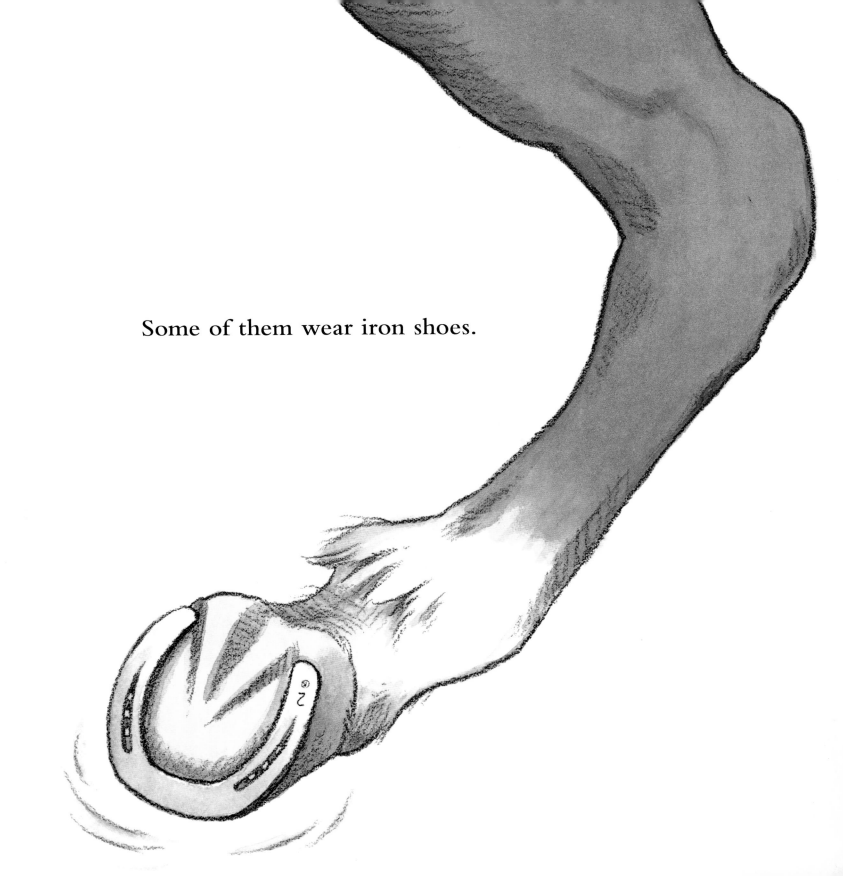

They like to graze on tasty grass—
that's how their lazy days all pass.

Cowboys' horses herd a cow.

Farmers' horses pull a plow.

Circus horses bow and prance,
pirouette, rear up, and dance.

Police ride horses on their beats,
clip-clop-clop down city streets.

Horses trot in grand parades,
manes and tails in fancy braids.

They swim a stream. Jump a wall.

Gallop after a polo ball.

Haul a wagon. Race on tracks.

Carry children on their backs.

Trit-trot-trot! Trit-trot-trot!
Clippity-clippity-clippity-clop!

In winter they can pull a sleigh—
jingle, *jingle*, all the way!

In stable, barn, or open shed,
straw or shavings make their bed.

They often sleep while standing up.
Have special pals—a goat or pup!

All year long, day by day,
horses work, rest, and play.

Popular horse breeds

Appaloosa

Arabian

Morgan

Paint

Palomino

Percheron

Quarter Horse

Saddlebred

Shetland Pony

Shire

Thoroughbred

Welsh Pony